5.00

FEATHER
TALES

Dinky Duck

David M. Sargent, Jr., and his friends live in Northwest Arkansas. His writing career began in 1995 with a cruel joke being played on his mother. The friends pictured with him are (from left to right), Vera, Buffy, and Mary.

Dave Sargent is a lifelong resident of the small town of Prairie Grove, Arkansas. A fourth-generation dairy farmer, Dave began writing in early December, 1990. He enjoys the outdoors and has a real love for birds and animals.

Dinky Duck

By

Dave Sargent

Illustrated by
Jane Lenoir

Ozark Publishing, Inc.
P.O. Box 228
Prairie Grove, AR 72753

Library of Congress cataloging-in-publication data

Sargent, Dave, 1941—
    Dinky Duck/by Dave Sargent ; illustrated by
Jane Lenoir.
        p. cm.
    Summary: Dinky Duck tries to ge Pokey Opossum
to be more prompt in seeking shelter from an approach-
ing tornado. Includes factul information about ducks.
        ISBN 1-56763-473-7 (cloth). — ISBN 1-56763-
475-5 (pbk
        [1. Behavior--Fiction. 2.Tornadoes--Fiction. 3.
Opossums--Fiction. 4. Ducks--Fiction.])
    I. Lenoir, Jane, 1950-ill. II Title.
    — ill. III. Title.
    PZ7.S2465 Di 2000
    [Fic]--dc21
                                        00-020093

Printed in the United States of America

Inspired by

watching the seemingly calm, cool and collected ducks on our ponds. They are such fun! But when we feed them, we always wear shoes!

Dedicated to

all students who love watching ducks
floating on a pond. They are not
afraid of people; they love to be fed,
and they talk a lot!

Foreword

Dinky Duck has a real job on her hands, teaching Pokey Opossum that being prompt is very important. Pokey learns his lesson when he almost loses his tail feathers in a bad tornado. Actually, he becomes quite a hero!

Contents

Dinky Duck

If you would like to have an author of The Feather Tale Series visit your school, free of charge, just call 1-800-321-5671 or 1-800-960-3876.

One

Run, Pokey! Run!

The dark cloud thundered and roared as it raced across the Arkansas countryside. Lightning streaked and jagged across the sky, momentarily lighting the whole area. Raindrops quickly collected and grew into big pools of water in low areas near the barn and outbuildings. Dinky Duck wriggled her tail as raindrops pelted her snowy white feathers.

"Swimming and diving in the big pond is great," she squealed, "but there's something special in a rain!"

"There is not," a small voice
drawled. "It's yucky and wet and
uncomfortable when I'm relaxing."

Dinky Duck jerked her head from side to side, trying to find the source of the complaint, but she did not see anyone nearby.

"My mama told me to hurry because of the weather, but I do hate to hurry," the little voice continued. "Mama yells at me all of the time because she thinks I'm too slow."

Dinky spun around in hopes of finding the little critter, but again she saw no one.

"Come out, come out, wherever you are," Dinky yelled.

Suddenly a big bolt of lightning struck an oak tree near Farmer John's house, and the following explosion of thunder seemed to shake the whole world.

"Whoa!" the little voice barked. "I don't like that! That was scary!"

This time, the duck looked up. A small furry body with hairless ears was hanging upside down from a tree limb by his skinny tail. Two big eyes stared downward as a gust of wind swung his little body to and fro.

"Who are you?" the duck asked. "And why are you hanging upside down during a thunderstorm?"

"My name is Pokey Opossum," he said. "And I'm hanging upside down because this is what I do best. I'm also real good at playing dead."

Dinky flapped her wings and glared up at the opossum. Water was dripping off her big orange bill as she tapped one webbed foot in the mud.

"Everyone has a special talent," Dinky Duck said sternly. "But most of us find the right way to use it. So far, Pokey Opossum, you seem to be a perfect lightning rod, hanging by your wet tail like that. Does your mama know where you are, little opossum?"

Pokey said, "She said to follow her home, but I wasn't in any hurry."

Suddenly Dinky saw Molly and
Farmer John running from the house.

"Hurry, Molly!" Farmer John yelled. "It's coming this way!"

They ran for the storm cellar. Pausing at the door, they stared at the storm cloud with frightened eyes.

Dinky turned to look. Her eyes widened in terror as she spotted a big black funnel cloud in the southwest.

"It's a tornado!" she screamed. "Run, Pokey! Run for low ground!"

Pokey shut his eyes and yawned. "I will. After I rest for a minute."

"Move quickly!" Dinky Duck shouted. "Your life depends on it!"

"My life depends on two things: sleeping when I'm tired and eating when I'm hungry," the little opossum drawled. "Nothing else is important. Mama tries to hurry me all the time, but I don't pay any attention to her. She's too picky."

"You will, little fellow," Dinky yelled over her shoulder, "after your tail feathers are blown off!"

"Oh, I don't have tail feathers," a faint voice replied with a giggle. "And even if I did, I have plenty of time to save them."

The duck muttered to herself as she waddled down the hill as fast as her little legs could carry her.

"That little pokey critter needs a good 'time out'!" Dinky grumbled.

"When things calm down around here, I'll find his mama, and we'll take care of that!"

When she reached a safer place, Dinky Duck turned and looked back at the tree. She gulped when she saw that the little critter was still dangling from the limb by his skinny tail.

Suddenly the wind and rain stopped. There was an eerie silence over the land for a brief moment. Then the duck heard the dreadful roar from the twister.

And seconds later, the tornado arrived on Farmer John place.

Two

Tornado!

The wind screamed and howled as it tore through to the middle of the farmyard. Dinky watched boards and debris spiral upward, then sail through the air and land in crumpled heaps on the muddy ground. She felt heartsick as she watched the roof of the hay barn tear apart and scatter in small pieces over the fields. Were her friends inside?

As suddenly as it had come, the tornado was gone. Dinky looked at the devastation and shook her head.

"Oh my," she cried. "Oh my. What should I do?"

She waddled in a circle for a full minute before screeching to a halt.

"Aren't you ashamed, cool headed Dink?" she scolded herself. "Wasting precious time in a nervous fit! Now go see if you can help some of your friends!"

Dinky's waddle back up the hill was fast and determined. She headed straight for a group of animals who had gathered near the damaged barn.

"Is everyone okay?" she asked.

"Yes, we think so," they said in unison.

"Good," Dinky Duck said with a smile. "If no one is hurt, we are very lucky."

Suddenly she whirled and yelled, "Has anyone seen a young possum?"

The group of animals shook their heads sadly.

One commented, "I saw you talking to little Pokey Opossum just before the storm hit, but I didn't see what happened to him."

"Oh," Dinky groaned. "If only he had been more prompt in seeking shelter, he would be here right now."

Low moans of sadness echoed through the little group.

Suddenly Dinky felt a tug on her right wing.

"I'm right here," a now familiar little voice said, "and I'm sorry that I worried you."

The duck turned toward the source and squealed, "Pokey! Is that really you? I thought you were blown into Lake Michigan or points beyond. I'm so happy to see that you survived the storm."

"I survived," Pokey said quietly,

"and I learned a good lesson in promptness, too" He sniffled and wiped a tear from his face with his front paw. "I'm sorry, Dinky Duck. I'll never be pokey again."

Dinky patted the little opossum

on the shoulder with one wing, and said, "What you mean is that you will be prompt." The duck grinned and winked as she added with a chuckle, "But, you will always be Pokey— Possum, that is!"

Suddenly the crowd heard the sound of vehicles racing up the drive. People jumped from their cars and trucks and ran toward Farmer John and Molly's damaged home.

"Molly!" yelled one of the women. "Where are you?"

"John!" a man shouted, "can you hear me? Talk to us so we can locate you beneath this debris!"

Dinky looked at the remains of the house and groaned.

"Whew," she whistled. "I'm sure glad they didn't stay inside."

The mob of concerned friends

were frantically digging amid the
remains of the house.

"They don't know where to look

for them," Dinky whispered. "Maybe I can let them know that Farmer John and Molly went to the storm cellar."

Dinky looked toward the underground shelter and gasped. The roof of the barn had settled on top of the door of the storm cellar.

"Oh my," she gasped. "Oh my,

oh my. They'll never find Molly and Farmer John under that awful mess. We must do something fast!"

"I have an idea," the duck said grimly, "but we will have to move fast. Pokey, this is what I need you to do . . ."

Three

Arrow on Target!

As Farmer John and Molly's friends continued searching through the rubble of the farmhouse, Dinky carefully positioned all the animals into the shape of an arrow with two rows of chickens forming the point. Then stepping back to survey her effort and sounding just a bit like a drill sergeant, she ordered each one to face the now hidden storm cellar. She shouted, "Move closer together! Get the point of the arrow on target! Tighten up that arrow shaft!"

Pokey Opossum stood quietly
as Dinky Duck nodded approval of
the work.

"Very good," the duck muttered. "Stand by, Pokey, it's your turn soon."

Moments later, Dinky shouted, "Fire one!"

The cows bellowed and bawled. The pigs squealed and oinked. The horse nickered, and the mule brayed. The geese honked, and the chickens squawked. Dinky ran as fast as she could toward the people who were looking for Farmer John and Molly. Flapping her big wings and quacking loudly, she raced in a circle around the group before turning back toward the concealed storm cellar.

"What is wrong with that crazy duck?" a man asked gruffly.

"Wait, listen!" a woman yelled. "The animals are all talking at once!"

"Look!" a fellow shouted as he ran toward the strangely arranged animals. "They're standing in the shape of an arrow!"

"Great!" Dinky Duck panted as she made another circle around the friends and and neighbors and raced to the point of the arrow.

"Now it's your turn, little Pokey. Ready? Okay . . . Get set . . . Now! Do your thing!" Dinky shouted.

Young Pokey Opossum ran up and down the arrow, then scrambled beneath the edge of the barn roof and hung by his skinny little tail.

The search party gathered near the mysterious menagerie, staring down the shaft of the arrow.

"I have never seen such an active opossum," one commented.

"I have never seen such strange behavior in any farm animals," another mumbled.

Suddenly, little Pokey fell to the ground, played dead for a moment, then returned to the hanging position beneath the roof.

"Fire three!" Dinky bellowed.

For the first time since 'Fire one', each and every critter stood perfectly still and quiet.

"This is really getting spooky," a lady whispered. "I'm going home."

"No, wait," one man muttered. "Listen. I hear something."

Muffled shouts from Molly and Farmer John could be heard drifting through the debris covering their underground shelter.

"The storm cellar! Help us!" both Farmer John and Molly called. "Please! We can't open the door!"

"Dismissed!" Dinky shouted as he waddled away from the activity.

Each and every cow, goose, chicken, horse, mule, pig, and sheep turned to silently follow him.

Dinky Duck glanced back and groaned, "Oh no. Pokey's still hanging upside down under the roof."

Before he had a chance to turn around to retrieve the little fellow, Pokey was scurrying toward him.

"Hey! Wait for me," he called. "I relapsed breifly from promtness!"

Dinky said with a smile. "You did a fine job of showing them where to look, Pokey. I'm proud of you."

Young Pokey Opossum looked down at his feet for a moment, then giggled nervously.

"Dinky Duck, would you mind telling my mama that I was prompt? If she knows that I'm learning to be prompt, it will make her happy."

Before Dinky had a chance to answer, a gentle voice said, "That isn't necessary, Pokey. I saw you, and you were wonderful."

"Mama!" Pokey Opossum said. "I'm so glad to see you! I'm sorry for being so slow in minding you. It's not gonna happen again, Mama. I promise!"

As mama and son stood there hugging one another, Dinky quietly waddled down the hill toward her favorite pond.

"I am proud of Pokey Opossum, too," she chuckled. "You know, that little fellow performed right on cue. I think he will be a very prompt and thoughtful son from this day forward. That tornado taught him a very good lesson. No siree. He won't be putting off doing what he's supposed to. . . . Will he?" Hmmm . . .

Four

Duck Facts

Duck is a name that applies to numerous species of a family of waterfowl. Ducks differ from geese and swans of the same family by their shorter necks and legs and other anatomical differences.

TORRENT DUCK

GARGANEY

Long-tailed Duck (or Old SQUAW)

Ducks live on all continents except Antarctica, and most of the world's islands. The legs of most ducks are placed far apart and toward the rear, making them awkward walkers but efficient swimmers. Their underplumage, or down, is buoyant and insulating, and is kept water-resistant by frequent preening with oil from a gland called the uropygial or preen gland, at the base of the tail feathers. Ducks have a spatula-like bill lined with bony notches for straining animal and plant matter from water.

Some island species cannot fly, but most ducks of northern continents are migratory. In a few species, the sexes are alike in color, but in most, males are much brighter.

Ducks have elaborate courtship displays. In North America, pairing-off takes place in the winter: hence, males wear their bright plumage in winter and briefly have a female-like "eclipse" plumage in summer. Nests of most species are on the ground, containing from 4 to 12 eggs, surrounded by down feathers plucked from the female's breast and belly.

Ducklings are able to swim and feed themselves soon after hatching. Some species, such as the wood duck of North America, nest in holes in trees and will accept artificial nest boxes. Their ducklings can jump from their nests without injury and take to the water soon afterwards.

BLUE-=WINGED TEAL

Distances covered by migrating ducks vary. One arctic duck, the spectacled eider, winters at sea off Alaska. Long-distance champion among American ducks is the blue-winged teal, which nests in most of North America and winters from the southern United States to Argentina.

There are more than a hundred species of ducks. Most familiar are the dabbling or surface-feeding ducks, which include the mallard.

Members of this group live primarily on fresh water, where they glean small aquatic animals and plants from the surface or from shallow bottoms they can reach without diving. The pochards, including the canvasback, nest on fresh water, but winter, often in very large flocks, both on inland lakes and along the coasts; they feed by diving. Another group of diving ducks, including the goldeneyes and the bufflehead, nest in tree holes. The mergansers are specialized for catching fish; the edges of their bills have sharp, tooth-like serrations for holding slippery prey. Most marine of the North American ducks are the eiders and scoters, which nest in the far north and winter predominantly at sea.

All except one breed of domestic duck are derived from the mallard, originally tamed in Eurasia. The exception is the muscovy duck, a large species of the American tropics. Wild muscovies are mostly black, but the most common domestic variety is white with knobby, naked red skin around the face and bill. It and the turkey are the only domestic birds that originated in the Americas.

J
Sargent